If I Were a Cow

Diane Wright

"I'm leaving," said the cow.
"Ready to go have some fun
On a two-week vacation
At the beach in the sun."

"But wait," said the pig.
"You can't leave right now.
While you are gone,
Who will be the cow?"

"Oh, please," said the pig.
"Please let it be me.
If I were the cow,
I'd be as happy as can be.

"Right now as a pig,
All I have is mud in my pen.
I stink and I smell,
And no one will be my friend.

"If I were a cow..."

"If I were a cow,
I could finally stand tall.
I'd have my own bed
In my very own stall.

"I wouldn't have to worry
About the way that I smell.
I'd be the center of the farm
And even wear the bell."

And so they decided
Right then and there,
That the pig would be the cow
With the farm in his care.

"But wait," said the pig,
"Not so fast, not just yet.
We now need a pig,
So who can we get?"

"Pick me, pick me,"
Said a voice they didn't know.
"I've travelled for days
From the land of ice and snow.

"As a penguin, I wear a suit
And must always look my best.
I can never have any fun
Because of how I'm dressed.

"If I were a pig..."

"If I were a pig,
I could jump and play
In the puddles and the mud
Every minute of every day.

"I'd be filthy and dirty
And love every minute,
Not caring about my suit
Or how I look in it."

The cow could go on vacation.
They had figured out how.
The penguin would be the pig,
And the pig would be the cow.

"But wait," said the penguin.
"We still have a hole.
Who will be the penguin
Down in the South Pole?"

"I'll help," said the camel.
"I'd love to lend a hand.
You see I spend my life
In the hot, hot sand.

"Each day I wither
Under the sun's hot blaze.
And when I need a drink,
I have to travel for days.

"If I were a penguin..."

"If I were a penguin,
Then anywhere I go,
I'd never see sand.
I'd only see snow.

"I'd be surrounded by water
And ice every day.
I'd sled, and I'd slide,
And I'd splash, and I'd play."

"That's it," they all said,
"The answer is clear.
The camel will be the penguin,"
They said with a cheer.

The penguin will be the pig
And the pig will be the cow.
They all worked together
To figure out how.

"There's just one thing to do
Before we reach our goal.
While I am the penguin,
Who will fill my role?"

"Let me be the camel,"
Said a voice from down low.
"I like being a turtle
But don't like being so slow.

"I'm never able to get
Very far from my home.
With these little legs,
There's only so far I can roam.

"If I were a camel...

"If I were a camel,
The first thing I'd do
Is travel to every
Place that I knew.

"I'd like all the sun.
I wouldn't care if it's hotter;
Because in my hump,
I'd have my own water."

And so they decided.
Everybody would win.
The turtle will be the camel,
And the camel will be the penguin.

The penguin will be the pig
And the pig will be the cow.
Everything was settled,
So the cow could leave now.

"I'm back," said the cow.
"I've got great stories to tell.
But first, how'd it go?
Did it all turn out well?"

"I thought you'd never come home.
Have you come to set me free?
This was so much more work
Than I thought it would be.

"Everyone wanted something.
I didn't get any rest.
Can I go back to being a pig?
It's what I like best."

"Me, too," said the penguin.
"At first it was a hoot.
But then I spent all my time
Washing my suit.

"I look really silly.
It's no fun at all.
Because my sleeves and my pants
Are two sizes too small."

"I'm ready to go back, too.
I've had enough of the cold.
I thought I would like it
From stories I'd been told.

"But my whole body chattered
From my head to my toes.
And now I have an igloo
From when my hump froze."

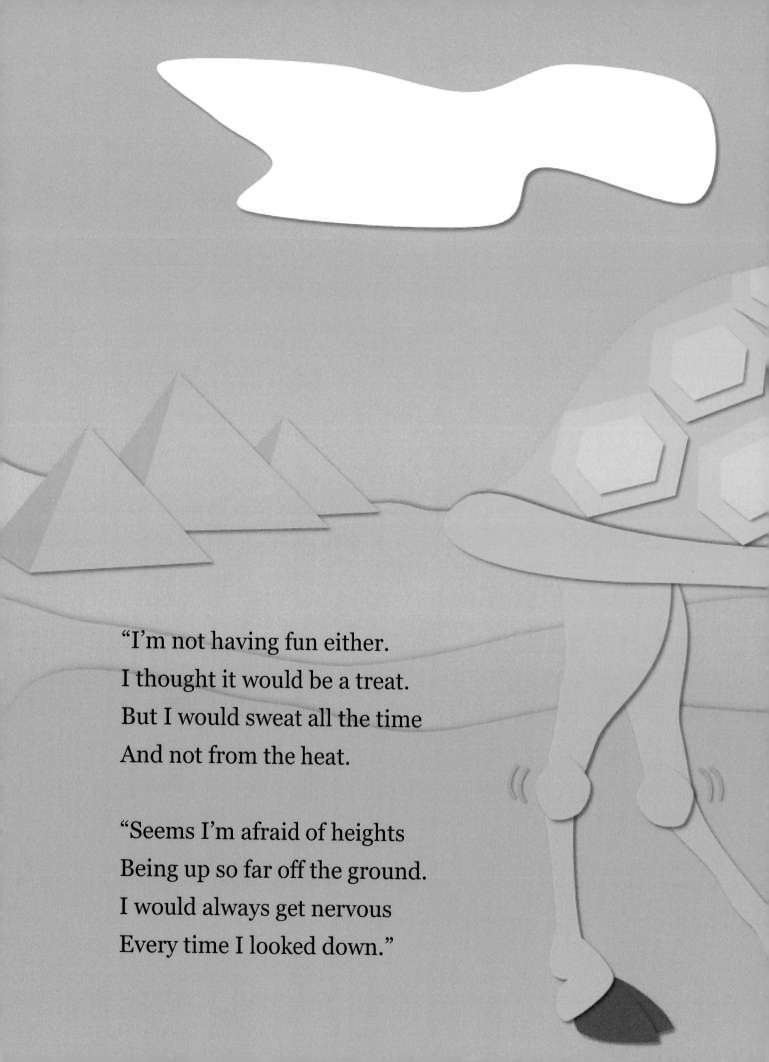

"I'm not having fun either.
I thought it would be a treat.
But I would sweat all the time
And not from the heat.

"Seems I'm afraid of heights
Being up so far off the ground.
I would always get nervous
Every time I looked down."

"I understand," said the cow.
"It's been an adventure for sure.
And now that I'm back,
We can return to how things were."

So the pig went back to his pen,
And the penguin was once again formal.
The camel returned to the desert,
While the turtle shrank down to normal.

And the cow was just
happy to be home.

The End

Made in the USA
Middletown, DE
08 July 2015